RED FOX

Don't forget the bacon!

Pat Hutchins

A Red Fox Book

Published by Random House Children's Books
61-63 Uxbridge Road, London W5 5SA

A division of The Random House Group Ltd
Addresses for companies within The Random House Group Limited
can be found at: www.randomhouse.co.uk/offices.htm

5 7 9 10 8 6

First published in the United Kingdom by The Bodley Head Children's Books 1976
Published in the US by Greenwillow Books, New York 1976

Red Fox edition 2002

Printed and bound in Singapore

The Random House Group Limited Reg. No. 954009

www.kidsatrandomhouse.co.uk

ISBN 978 0 099 41398 1

For Ben and Jeb Kidd

Six fat legs,
a cape for me,
a pound of pears,
and don't forget
the bacon.

41 The Cake Shop 41

fresh cream
cakes

41